To us

First published in the United States and Canada in 2015
by Lemniscaat USA LLC • New York
Distributed in the United States by Lemniscaat USA LLC • New York

Cataloging-in-publication data is available.
ISBN 978-1-935954-08-8 (Hardcover)
Printed in the United States by Worzalla, Stevens Point, Wisconsin
First U.S. Edition
www.lemniscaatusa.com

Ingrid & Dieter Schubert

There Is a Crocodile Under my Bed

What's under there?
Sophie notices Carl right away.

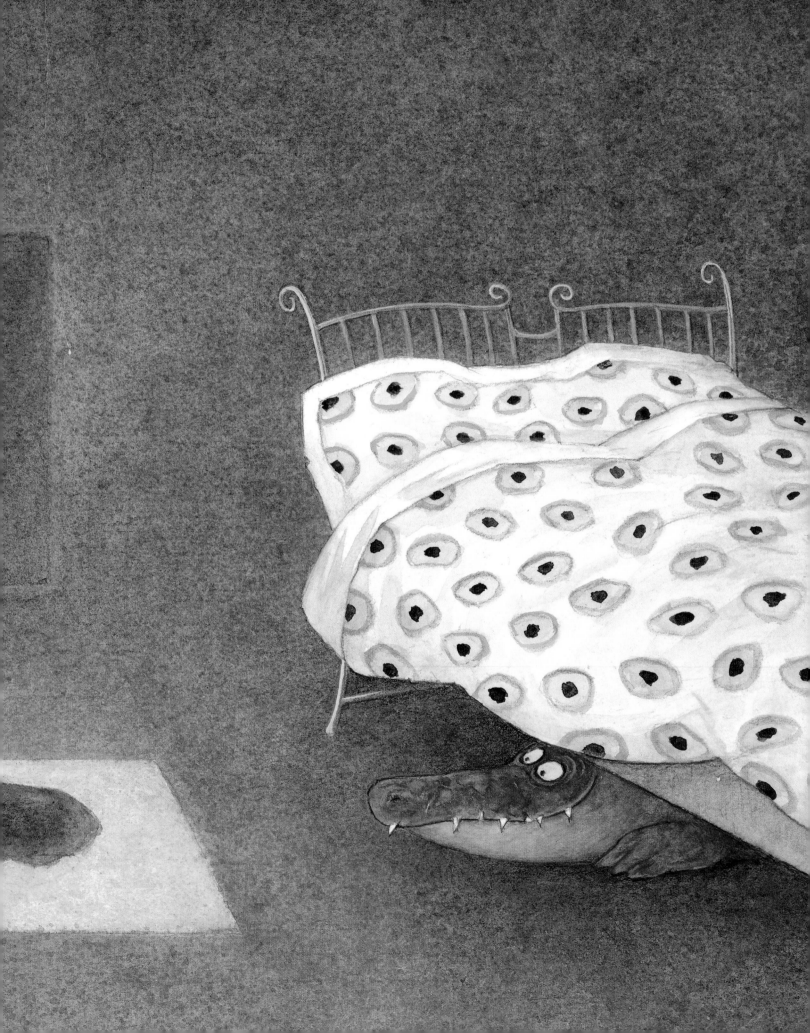

Quickly, Sophie slams the door behind her.
"There's a crocodile under my bed!" she calls out.
"And I am not scared at all!" she adds.

But Carl is....

He tries to hide.
"Get off my dresser," Sophie demands.

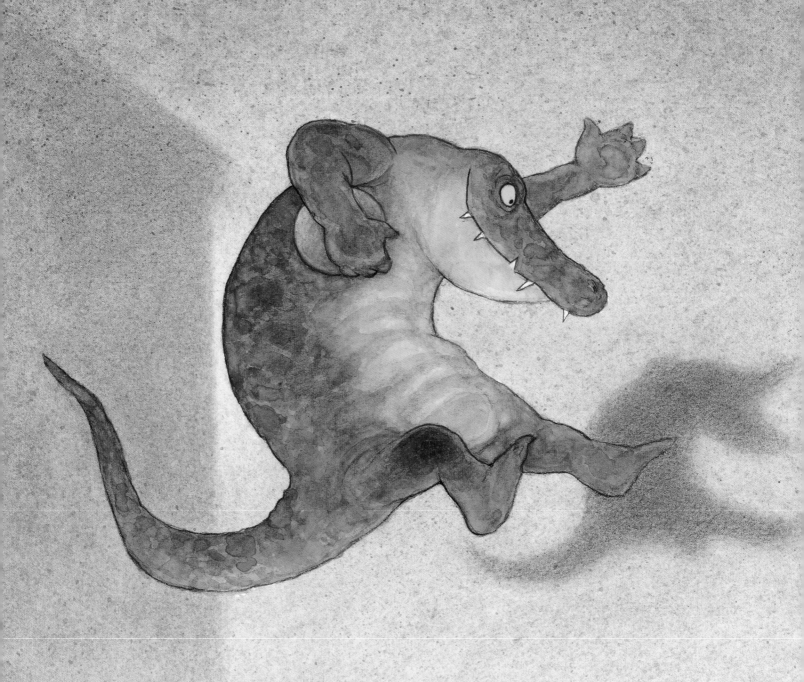

"Do you dare to jump through the hoop?"

Carl is as tame as a dog.

The two perform tricks until they're breathless.

"Stay awake!" Sophie orders. "I'm hungry."

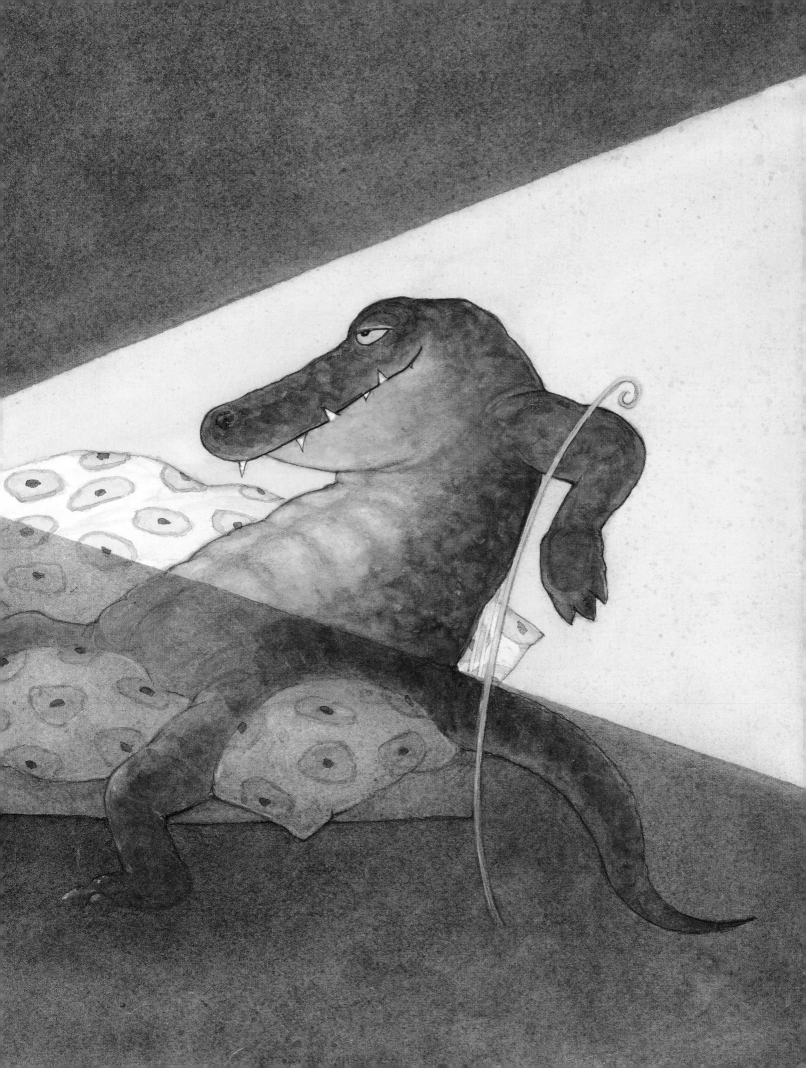

Carl gets to work immediately.

They flip at least a thousand pancakes.

Carl spots the empty egg cartons and gets a fantastic idea.
He shows Sophie how to cut and paste them.

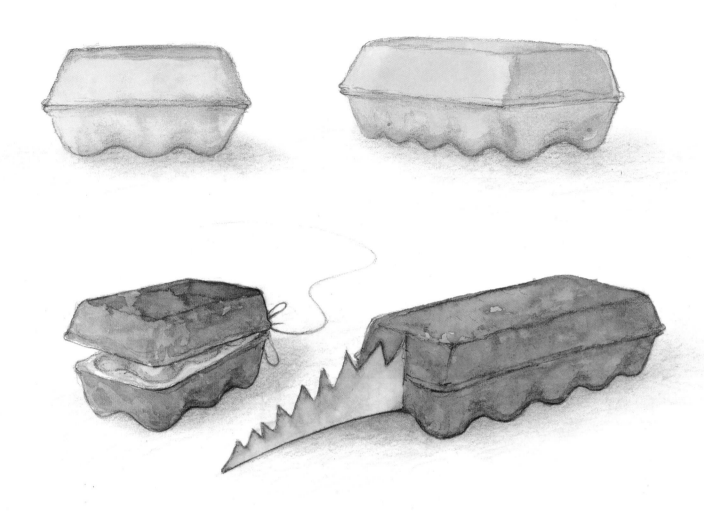

An egg-carton-crocodile!

Now *that's* scary looking!

Carl is one big mess of paint, glue, and maple syrup.
"Into the tub with you!" Sophie says.

Luckily, Carl is not afraid of water.

"That was fun!" Sophie says.
"Now I want a story."

Carl tells all about his pranks…

about his adventures…

about his crocodile business…

until Sophie is fast asleep.

As quiet as a mouse, Carl tiptoes out.